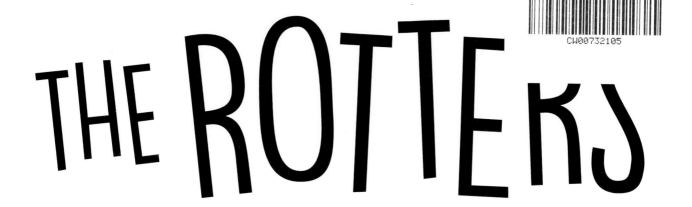

THE ROTTERS

Cazzie Phillips

Illustrated by Agnès Ernoult

Seadragon

For my family. You're jawsome!
— CP

To my kids, listen to the SCG and
don't let the Rotters get you!
— AE

First published in 2023 by Seadragon

Text and illustrations copyright © Cazzie Phillips, 2023

ISBN 978-1-7384530-0-9
Also available as an eBook
978-1-7384530-1-6

info@seadragon.co.uk

Seadragon

Meet the Rotters

The Rotters are based on real bacteria that live in our mouths from birth, called streptococcus mutans.

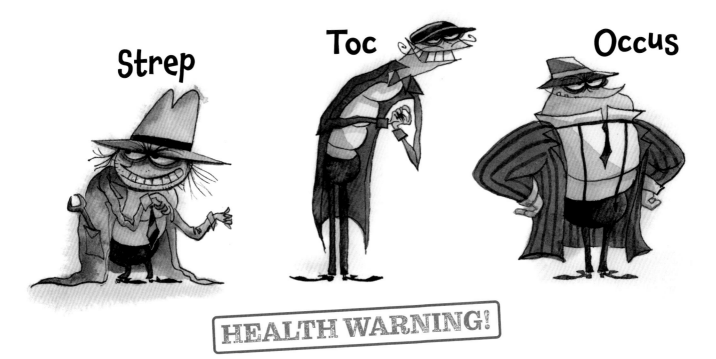

Strep

Toc

Occus

HEALTH WARNING!

You may be relieved to hear that
the bacteria in this story are *not* drawn to scale!

Mutans

Plaque

Tartar

For more information about real Rotters,
visit **www.therotters.club**

Finn Greedyfeet loved to eat snacks and sweets,
but he never wanted to clean his teeth.

What he didn't know, was in the dirt,
a gang of greedy tooth fiends lurked . . .

There hid Strep, Toc, Occus and Mutans,
revolting beasts with revolting plans.

"This boy's mucky mouth is the perfect spot!"

"To binge on old cake, sugary drinks and chocs!"

"Yummy!" said Occus, rubbing his tummy.

"Let's feast on his teeth, then make them rot!"

Finn had been warned many times to keep his teeth clean,
  but he was too busy playing, and far from keen.

"I don't believe sweeties make holes!" he'd say.
Well, not until the Rotters went too far one day...

"Ouch!"

Finn screeched, as pain shot up his cheek,
and all his friends turned to see who'd shrieked.

No medicine or treats could stop the aching,
so off to the dentist he was taken.

10

That's where the Rotters were stopped in their tracks,
by a spotlight that caught them right in the act!

Behind the bright beam was Dr Carey,
  a friendly dentist, who the Rotters found scary.

    In she peered to see what was lurking.
      "Decay, Finn, is why your teeth are hurting.
    I'll clean them today to take the ache away,
      but then it's up to you to brush twice a day."

        "But what . . ." asked Finn " . . . if I forget to brush?
          Or I'm too busy playing, or I'm in a rush?"

"I'm sorry to say, there's no other way.
  Not brushing your teeth will lead to decay.
**My next patient stopped, and in crept the rot,
  and now Tim's toothless, all because he forgot!"**

    Dr Carey took Finn to meet Toothless Tim.
      "He'll tell you exactly what happened to him."

Tim stood in the waiting room, thin as a bean,
with the scariest grin Finn had ever seen!

"I ate too many sweets, and never cleaned my teeth.
Now I smell like mouldy cheese whenever I breathe!
I eat through a straw, and drool like a dog,
I got no teeth left, 'coz the Rotters got the lot."

Finn gawped. He gasped. He asked, agog,
"What are . . . *Rotters?*
Do they live in your—"

Finn's mum quickly cut in, "Well, we'd better run.
Thanks Dr Carey. See you in six months?"

The dentist nodded and Tim waved goodbye.
"Just don't do what I did, kid!" he called in reply.

All the way home, Rotters preyed on Finn's mind.
   Were there beasts that stole teeth and lived on grime?
He didn't want to end up like Toothless Tim,
   dribbling like a baby with a Halloween grin.

But from that day on, did Finn brush
each day? Of course he didn't!
It was more fun to play!

That's when Strep, Toc, Occus and Mutans,
  swiftly regrouped with a wicked plan.

"We'll tempt him ..." said Strep, "... to our Sugar Lair!"

"And make sure," Toc grinned, "he gets stuck in there!"

"Then!" cried Occus. "We'll have a home forever!"

"Oh joy!" sang Mutans. "We're so jaw-droppingly clever!"

Finn awoke to find the fiends in his room,
but he was more spellbound
by the scrumptious food!

"It's all yours!" Strep urged.
"Don't hold back!"

"Just for you!" Toc winked.
"Such yumptious snacks!"

The Rotters all grinned with wide, hopeful smiles,
as Finn gazed at the feast that went on for miles.

He drooled over ice creams and sweet jelly goo,
surely, he could lose just one tooth, or two . . . ?

18

"Let's do it!" cried Finn, and dived into the sludge,
past cream cake castles and towers of fudge,
into a wood of pink candyfloss trees,
where lollies swayed temptingly in the breeze.

But just as he reached for slices of cake,
Finn heard shouting from the marshmallow lake.

"STOP!"

"Don't let them trick you with all their sweets!
Those filthy Rotters will destroy your teeth!"

Three skilful surfers sailed smoothly to shore.

"I'm Brusha."

"I'm Floss."

"And my name's Flor!"

20

"We're the Sugar Crush Gang."

"With a tooth-saving plan!"

"You don't want to hang with Strep, Toc,
  Occus and Mutans!"

"You've got to paste those squatters,
  and look after your choppers!
Or you won't get them back from those thieving Rotters!"

"**Too late!**" Mutans cut in. "Finn's our next Toothless Tim!
  And he'll soon have the same irresistible grin!"

"We'll have his canines for breakfast, and incisors
  for brunch!"

"The muck on his teeth will make a delicious lunch!"

Brusha raised a bristle and coolly shook her brush.

"Don't be so sure of that! **It's time to sugar crush!**"

Flor was first to aim, squirting hosepipes of paste,
which burst like minty snowballs in each Rotter's face!

Floss looped in next to flick off clumps of waste,
as the Rotters raced to stop their snacks flying into space!

Brusha blitzed East Molar Street and sprayed Incisor Mews,
turning them from filthy slums to pearls with gleaming hues!

Finn stared agog, not knowing what to do,
when he saw **more strange beasts** loom from the goo!

"I'm Plaque," one cooed.

"Me too!"

"Me too!"

"Me too!"

"I'm Tartar. Rock hard, and I stick like glue!"

"It's true!"

"It's true!"

"It's true!"

"Finn! Don't just stand there!" Flor gave him a nudge.
"Go grab a brush and start pasting those slugs!"

But Plaque flung a net, and caught Finn
in her trap.

"**Help!**" he yelled, as Tartar waddled
to attack.

"Use this!" Floss cried, tossing a
Sugar Crush case, filled with all the
tools he needed to escape.

Quickly, Finn scrubbed his way out of their prison,
to join the gang on their grime-busting mission.
Together, they pasted, and brushed, and flossed.
The Rotters went flying and soon knew they'd lost.

"You may have won this time, but we'll be back!"

And off they squirmed to find a new home with snacks.

The Sugar Crush Gang and Finn all high-fived.

"Great job! Pleased to see your gnashers survived!"

"Sun's coming up," said Flor. "It's time to leave.
    More kids are whinging about cleaning their teeth."

With dazzling grins, the gang waved and cheered,
    and through a white mist they all disappeared!

Finn woke up with a start, and scanned his room.
Were there still Rotters lurking in the gloom?
But no signs remained. Not one blob of paste,
until he spotted **the Sugar Crush case!**

From that day on,
   Finn never forgot
to paste and brush off that
   rotten lot.

At his next check-up,
   just six months later,
Dr Carey said,
   "Your teeth couldn't be greater!
There are some lovely
   new ones coming through.
Take good care of them,
   and they'll take care of you"

As Finn bounded out, Toothless Tim headed in,
proudly beaming with a **brand-new grin!**

"Don't be fooled," laughed Tim, pulling out his dentures.
"These don't make up for my misadventures!

You gotta keep up the fight twice a day,
'coz those Rotters will never go away!"

With the Sugar Crush tools and all he now knew,
Finn grinned knowingly, **"I already do!"**

Glossary

Some of the words used in the story may be new to you? Here are a few of them to get your teeth round. See which ones you already know, or try guessing what they mean before you read the definition!

agog (adj.)   This is another way of saying astonished or amazed, with a sense of shock.

bacteria (n.)   Groups of single-celled microorganisms found in every habitat on earth. Some live in, or on, other organisms including plants, animals and humans. There are approximately 10 times as many bacterial cells as human cells in our bodies. But more than 99% are helpful to our bodies, and less than 1% are harmful.

binge (v.)   Doing an excessive amount of something, like eating too much all-in-one go!

candyfloss (n.)   A British word for spun sugar also known as 'cotton candy' in the US.

caries (n.)   Another way of saying tooth decay, or describing cavities (holes, cracks or gaps).

choppers/ gnashers/ pearly whites (n.)   These are all informal words used to describe teeth. Can you imagine why we use these words?

dentures (n)   Removeable false teeth, that can be made of different materials, such as plastic, porcelain or metal.

gob (n.)   This is a British slang word for mouth, which can be onsidered a bit impolite. It's also used in Australia and New Zealand. This word isn't actually mentioned in the story. Can you find where 'gob' might go?

Glossary continued

misadventures (n.)   Unplanned situations that go wrong or turn out badly, usually with unexpected or negative consequences, such as Toothless Tim losing his teeth because he ate too much sugar and didn't clean it off.

paste (v./ n.)   This word can be used in different ways.
In the story it's used as –
i) a shortened form to describe toothpaste
ii) as the verb 'to paste': a British slang term that means 'to be heavily defeated', just like the Rotters were defeated by the SCG!
It can also be used to mean 'to glue together'.

plaque (n.)   Sticky biofilm made of food debris and saliva that forms a slippery net over our teeth and traps grime.

squat (v./ n.)   (n.) A place where someone lives without the owner's permission.
(v.) Describes a crouching movement close to the ground

squatter (n.)   Someone who lives in a place without the owner's permission.

streptococcus mutans (n.)   Bacteria that lives in our mouths from birth and contributes to tooth decay.

tartar (n.)   Hardened formations of plaque.

whinge (v.)   A verb that describes a way of complaining persistently in a particularly annoying manner! Do you know anyone who does that...?

Cazzie Phillips

Cazzie Phillips cut her teeth at the BBC as a broadcast journalist. She has since worked in multimedia communications, business and production for nearly thirty years. With two boys of her own, she's passionate about children's health, education and wellbeing, and honoured to be Chair of the Peter Le Marchant Trust. Cazzie's also partial to dark chocolate, but don't tell the Rotters!

"Heartfelt thanks to family and friends for your time and support during the writing of this book. You know who you are! Much love."

Find out more at

www.therotters.club   @cazziephillips   facebook.com/cazziephillips

Agnès Ernoult

Agnès Ernoult is a children's book illustrator living in France. She loves to illustrate stories that are fun and imbued with a touch of magic. She creates all sorts of crazy, whimsical characters using her nib and her watercolour palette. Her work has been published in Australia, France, the US and the UK. Agnès believes that every tale she illustrates is akin to a journey into a new world, filled with deeper messages that children and parents can discover together. When she's not painting, Agnès loves cooking odd recipes using wild greens from her garden.

Find out more @agnesernoult